THE FUTURE OF CHRISTMAS

Christopher White

Christmas is coming.

SANTA IS STRESSED.

Millions of letters and no
time to rest!

"Lapland has to change, and quick. The number of children, we can't predict. There's only one Santa and not many elves. We simply must look after ourselves."

"Bernard, what do you suggest?"

"TECHNOLOGY, SANTA. We have to invest."

...and cars drive themselves! The world's gone **BERSERK**.

There's lots of technology that we can use. It's the key to survival — we can't refuse!"

"Kids could use phones for their Christmas lists. We'll build an app to do just this.

Millions of letters? Not anymore. The app could be The Christmas Store.

All of the presents you've ever seen. The kids can choose them by tapping the screen.

We can see all of the lists online. No letters to open –

WE'LL SAVE LOADS OF TIME."

Santa is keen on Bernard's ideas.

"EXCELLENT THINKING, BUT WON'T IT TAKE YEARS?"

"Maybe one year if we work really hard.
We'll leave kids a note in this year's Christmas card,

explaining how next year, things will be better.
Download Santa's App – no need for a letter."

ONE
YEAR
LATER...

Merry Christmas

The plan has worked; most lists are online.
Santa is pleased, they've saved loads of time.

"Do the other elves have
work to do?

ARE **THEY**
BEING **GOOD?**

I'VE **ONLY**
SEEN
YOU."

No need to worry, it's all in hand. A technology Winter Wonderland.
"Santa, take a well-earned rest. We'll put these gadgets to the test."

They wait for all of the
drones to come back.

"Elves, fetch my sleigh and
my giant sack."

Santa makes a dashing flight, reaching the houses before it gets light.

Christmas disaster averted.

PHEW!

The kids won't even have a clue.

"I think we should build a

ROBOT ME!"

Printed in Poland
by Amazon Fulfillment
Poland Sp. z o.o., Wrocław